Pirate Patch

and the

Abominable Pirates

In which the dauntless Pirate Patch and Granny Peg sail to the far north and discover two abominable . . . pirates?

For Matthew
R.I.

For Rose
N.R.

Reading Consultant: Prue Goodwin, Lecturer in Literacy and
Children's Books at the University of Reading

ORCHARD BOOKS
338 Euston Road, London NW1 3BH
Orchard Books Australia
Hachette Children's Books
Level 17/207 Kent Street, Sydney NSW 2000

First published by Orchard Books in 2009

Text © Rose Impey 2009
Illustrations © Nathan Reed 2009

A CIP catalogue record for this book is available from the British Library

ISBN 978 1 84362 981 8 (hardback)
ISBN 978 1 84362 989 4 (paperback)

1 3 5 7 9 10 8 6 4 2
Printed in China

Orchard Books is a division of Hachette Children's Books,
an Hachette Livre UK company.
www.hachettelivre.co.uk

Pirate Patch

and the

Abominable Pirates

ROSE IMPEY · NATHAN REED

ORCHARD BOOKS

For once Patch and his
capable crew were *not* in
search of adventure.
It was far too hot for that.

Creeping Crayfish!

Instead Patch decided to do
a spot of fishing. Granny Peg,
Pierre and Portside decided to
do a spot of sleeping.

THE LITTLE PEARL

Only the sound of their snoring broke the peace and quiet. As far as Patch could see, there was only sea.

But suddenly he spotted another ship on the horizon!

It was Bones and Jones.
Patch was in no mood to meet
that *villainous* pair today.

Patch slipped *The Little Pearl*
into a handy cove until the
coast was clear.

By the time they set sail again,
the blue sky was turning grey.
A storm was blowing up.

The Little Pearl was tossed about on massive waves like a matchbox.

The whole crew held on tightly.

Patch and his ship were blown miles off course – further north than they had ever been before.

It was getting colder by the minute.

Granny Peg was busy knitting up
a storm of scarves, hats and gloves
to keep them all from freezing.

In no time they were surrounded by huge icebergs. Pierre kept lookout while Patch steered the little ship between them.

Caw! Caw!

Staggering Starfish!

PEARL

They needed to find
somewhere to shelter,
away from the icy winds.

At last Pierre spotted the place.

16

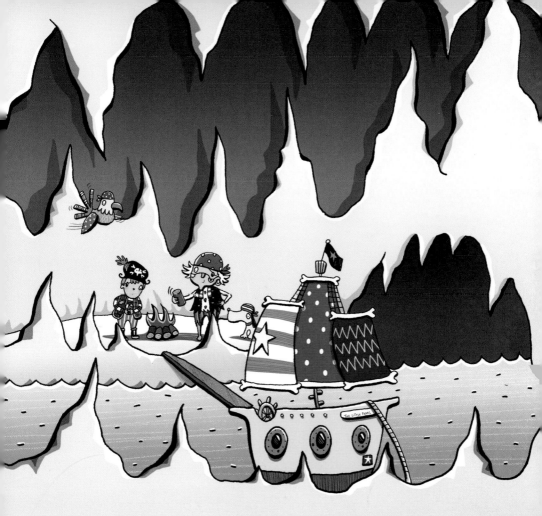

Patch and his crew dropped
anchor. They left the ship and
quickly made a fire to warm
themselves up.

It was quite cosy, sitting there with mugs of cocoa, while Peg told them the story of the *Abominable Snowman*.

"They say he's as high as a house and as wide as a whale!" whispered Peg. "No one's ever seen him – but his footprints are gigantic."

19

Patch was far too brave
a little pirate to be really
scared by one of Peg's stories.

But when an icicle melted and ran down his neck, Patch couldn't help squealing. The sound echoed all round the cave!

Patch's squeal made the rest of the crew feel nervous. They felt even more nervous when they saw a trail of *gigantic* footprints.

It led into a dark corner of the cave. Suddenly out of the darkness they heard heavy footsteps coming their way.

They were coming closer . . .
and closer . . .
Patch didn't *want* to believe
Peg's story.

But when he saw two huge, white shapes coming towards them, Patch yelled, "Let's get out of here!"

Back on the ship, Patch tried
to put on a brave face.
Abominable Snowmen! He'd
been caught out like that
once before.

THE LITTLE PEARL

"It was probably a pair of abominable *pirates*," he laughed. And Patch could guess which scurvy pair, too!

So he was rather surprised when he got back to the harbour to find his two old enemies already there.

What a scorcher!

Bones and Jones didn't look
as if they'd spent all day in
the far north.
"So who were those two scary
monsters?" Patch wondered.

Later when Peg asked what
kind of bedtime story Patch
wanted, he shivered, and
said, "Not one of your
scary ones."

His head was already full
of *abominable snowmen* and
abominable pirates. And that
was quite enough – even for
a brave little pirate like Patch!

★ Pirate Patch ★

ROSE IMPEY   NATHAN REED

All priced at £8.99

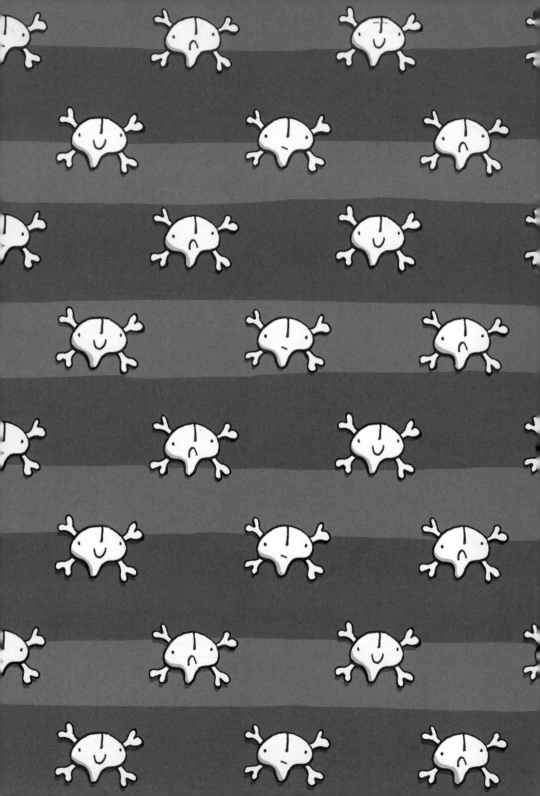